HOOKED

HOOKED

TALKING ABOUT ADDICTIONS

BY ELAINE LANDAU

The Millbrook Press
Brookfield, Connecticut

Library of Congress Cataloging-in-Publication Data
Landau, Elaine.
Hooked: talking about addictions / by Elaine Landau.
p.   cm.
Includes bibliographical references and index.
Summary: Describes a wide variety of addictions, from substance
abuse to compulsive behaviors, and explores some of the causes and
treatments that are available.
ISBN 1-56294-469-X
1. Substance abuse—United States—Juvenile literature.   2. Drug
abuse—United States—Juvenile literature.   3. Alcoholism—United
States—Juvenile literature.   4. Compulsive behavior—United States—
Juvenile literature.   [1. Compulsive behavior.   2. Substance
abuse.]   I. Title.
HV4999.2.L36   1994
362.29—dc20   94-41680   CIP   AC

Cover photograph courtesy of Mimi Forsyth
Monkmeyer Press Photo Service
Photographs courtesy of The Image Works: pp. 8 (© Michael Siluk),
14 (© Esbin-Anderson), 28 (© W. Marc Bernsau), 34 (Harriet Gans);
Impact Visuals: pp. 17 (© 1993 Andrew Lichtenstein); AP/Wide
World Photos: pp. 21, 48; Monkmeyer Press Photo Service: pp. 24
(Irene Bayer), 26 (Arlene Collins), 31 (Arlene Collins), 39 (Lois
Zenkel), 50 (Rhoda Sidney); UPI/Bettmann: p. 45.

CONTENTS

ONE
WHAT IS ADDICTION?

Lincoln School Library

JERRY) **AGE 17**

"I started drinking in the seventh grade. I did it because my friends drank at parties and it was a cool thing to do. Usually, it was beer. We'd get it from our parents' supply or pool our money and have an older kid buy it for us. Sometimes we'd pay him to do it; other times somebody would just help us out.

"We'd have contests at parties to see who could chug the most before throwing up. It sounds silly, but winning was important to look macho. Besides having a good time with my buddies, I realized how different booze made me feel. It gave me the courage to talk to any girl. I was suddenly easygoing and confident.

"After a while, my friends and I started drinking after school. We'd meet at one another's house when nobody else was home. Most of the time everybody came to my place because both my parents work on Wall Street in the city [New York City]. They have this thing about impressing one another

and their friends with how successful they are. They leave early in the morning and don't get back until real late. Even when they were home, they barely knew what was going on 'cause they were always on the phone doing business. They liked it when my friends were over because they thought I was happily occupied. That way, they didn't have to feel guilty about ignoring me.

"I felt fine too. Beer was like a super strength aspirin for me. When I felt lonely or unimportant, it took all the pain away fast. When I drank, I didn't care if it mattered to my parents whether or not I was alive.

"My friends and I used to put vodka in jello to make jello shots. We'd gulp them down in front of my Mom and Dad and they didn't know what was going on. They thought we were just having jello. Sometimes I felt high. Other times I felt numb. I'd stumbled on a way to block out feeling left out.

"I also drank by myself at home. If my parents were around, I'd do it in my room or the basement. I don't recall exactly when I started drinking at school, but after a while I'd bring the stuff with me in a thermos bottle to get through the day. That's where I got caught. I lied to everybody and told them I never drank before, but I started to realize how much I needed to drink. It had become too hard to stay sober for very long."

Peer pressure to drink can be overwhelming for teens.

MARK / AGE 14

"I always said I'd never do drugs because I know it's really dumb. I've seen kids who were strung out and I don't want to be like them. At my old school not many people were into that stuff. Most of us signed a pledge the principal passed out promising to steer clear of it.

"But everything changed when we started middle school. All of a sudden signing an anti-drug pledge wasn't cool. Now everybody did whatever felt good. Michael, a kid in my English class, told me about huffing. I'd seen kids doing it but I didn't know it had a name or what it felt like. People at school inhaled stain repellent, spray paint, gasoline or diesel fuel, typing correction fluid, nail polish remover, even cooking sprays. Anything they could get their hands on to get high.

"I was with Mike and two of his friends when I tried it. They were the experts, but it wasn't hard to do. You just spray the stuff on a rag, hold it to your face and breathe in deeply. The smell's always bad and it makes your head reel, but after a few times you don't mind anymore.

"Before long, I was huffing about five or six days a week. I liked the feeling, so I'd do it both by myself and with Michael and his friends. It was okay because I still wasn't doing drugs or anything. Sometimes the stuff I needed was lying around the house.

"My parents have never heard of huffing but my sister caught me at it a few times. She's a nag and says I'm taking too many risks. That's because Mike told her how I spray the stuff on my sleeve so I can inhale it in class and at the mall. I even did it in church once and nobody caught on. It makes doing what I have to do easier.

"But my sister still always points out whenever somebody we know gets into trouble because of something he inhaled. Cody, Michael's best friend, huffed a lot—he'd do it during most of the school day. Cody was a real good student, but everybody knew something was wrong when he started failing tests and couldn't remember things. He also used to be a great athlete. But this year he didn't go out for sports and sometimes he could hardly breathe when he ran.

"About two months ago Cody collapsed in the hall on his way to class. A couple of teachers rushed over to help him and an ambulance was called. The school nurse did CPR but somebody said Cody still wasn't breathing and that his heart had stopped.

"The next day we heard that Cody's heart and lungs failed a couple of times before his kidneys shut down. He had permanent lung and liver damage and almost no brain activity. Somebody said that if Cody pulled through he'd be a vegetable because he'd been without oxygen for too long. He didn't pull through, though. The doctors said his official cause of death was inhalant overdose.

"After Cody died we had an assembly at school on the dangers of huffing. A doctor and nurse came and said a lot of scary things. The principal announced that counselors were available for anyone who felt he couldn't stop huffing or needed to talk about what happened to Cody. My sister said I should go, but I don't need to. Cody's death was a fluke. No one expected him to die. My friends and I may be into huffing but we're not addicts. Addicts can't live without their booze or drugs. Cigarette lighter fluid is not the same as beer or cocaine. It's not illegal. Like I said, I don't do drugs."

VICKI / AGE 16

"I always wanted a good body so I could wear a leotard and tight miniskirt and have boys turn around to look at me. But I also wanted a strong, athletic body. I always admired female dancers and swimmers. They were all muscle—no fat. I wanted to be like them and thought jogging and aerobics could help me get that way. I could lose weight and tone my thighs.

"I started getting up at five in the morning to jog before school. After school or in the early evening, I worked out at the gym. At first, things were great. I wished I'd started exercising earlier. I couldn't believe that I could actually eat more and lose weight.

"Exercise made me feel strong and powerful. Afterwards I was ready to take on just about anything. Within months, everyone said I looked better. I also thought exercise made me more alert—it tuned up my brain. I think I did better on tests after running a few miles in the morning.

"Working out helped me in other ways. When things weren't going right at school, or with my friends or a boy I liked, it took my mind off the problem and gave me something to do. Maybe I couldn't change other things in my life, but I could always exercise.

"At first my parents praised me for being so disciplined about working out. Dad always said that people who stick to things get ahead. He told his friends how I got up extra early on Sundays to run a full 8 miles (13 kilometers) before church. When it got colder, my folks turned our basement into a mini-gym with a treadmill, exercise bike, and weights.

"But about then the trouble began. Since it was so easy for me to exercise at home, I spent more and more time in our basement gym. Those were hours I used to spend studying. Sometimes I'd read while on the treadmill or exercise bike. But most of the time I'd just put on music and work out.

"I swore I'd never skip an exercise period I planned for myself. But after a few months, it was hard to stick to my goal. When I didn't do well in French, my mother blamed it on the time I spent in the basement. To make peace, I studied after school, but set my alarm clock so I'd wake up in the middle of the night to secretly exercise. Once my mother found me on the treadmill at two o'clock in the morning and unplugged the machine. She threatened to throw it out if I used it again during the night.

"Things really exploded over Christmas. Every year we go to my grandmother's farm in Vermont for the holidays. The problem was that there wasn't a gym for miles around. I begged my parents to let me stay at a friend's house, but they refused. They said I wasn't going to disappoint my grandmother and disrupt the family at Christmas just so I could run on a treadmill like a harried rat.

"That left me no choice but to jog while we were at my grandmother's. But on Christmas Eve, when I came back after midnight from an hour and a half run, my parents were at the door to greet me. I thought they'd gone to bed, and I hadn't counted on them realizing that I'd been out. They didn't yell. My mother's eyes just got watery and my father looked down at the floor and said in a sad voice, 'Vicki, you've got a problem.'"

Vicki's father was right. She did have a problem. And while at first glance Vicki's problem may not seem to be the same as Jerry's or Mark's, it actually is. Whether through exercise, the

use of inhalants, or drinking, these young people have lost control of their lives. Their feelings and behaviors are driven by forces outside themselves. Each is suffering from an addiction.

At times, experts have debated how to determine whether problem behaviors should be classified as habits, compulsions, or addictions. While definitions vary among authorities, the distinctions described below are frequently used.

A habit is a behavior repeated so often that the person performs it without thinking about it. People aren't born with habits—these are learned behaviors and can either be good or bad. Nail biting is an example of an undesirable habit. A compulsion is an act or ritual that an individual feels compelled to perform. Compulsive acts may seem useless or irrational, but someone with a compulsion experiences an irresistible urge to engage in that behavior. Continually washing your hands even when they are clean is a compulsion. An addiction is a powerful and all-consuming need for a substance or a form of behavior that becomes destructive.

CHANGING
DEFINITIONS

Addictions were once thought of only in terms of dependence on a substance such as alcohol and other drugs. People such as Jerry, who took large amounts of these substances and devel-

Even healthy activities such as exercise can be harmful when carried to an extreme.

[15]

oped an intense mental and physical need for them, were considered addicts. As their bodies became used to the substances or developed a "tolerance," they needed to take increasingly larger quantities. If they suddenly stopped taking the drugs, they experienced severe "withdrawal" symptoms. Emotionally, they might feel as if they were falling apart. Physical reactions could include severe nausea, vomiting, changes in heart rate and blood pressure, trembling, sweating, mental confusion, and hallucinations.

In recent years, the concept of addiction has been broadened by some experts to include behaviors that people pursue beyond the usual limits. Among activities that people pursue to an extreme are excessive eating, dieting, playing sports, shopping, exercising, collecting, and gambling, to name a few. Some researchers believe that in certain circumstances people can become addicted to almost any kind of activity. Addictions of this type can start as habits that seem harmless or even good. However, when carried to extremes, even a highly regarded activity can turn into a destructive one that eventually takes its toll on the person and those closest to him or her.

With any type of addiction, in the first phase the person becomes mentally preoccupied with the substance or the form of behavior. He or she often finds it difficult to think about anything else. This is when the second phase of addiction begins: the overwhelming need to act on these feelings. The person may drive compulsively, exercise or diet constantly, or take drugs daily. According to Eileen Correa, program director of the Ochsner Addictive Behavior Treatment Program in New Orleans, Louisiana, behaviors can be classified as addictions when the "Three C's" are present:

Street kids hang out on New York City's Lower East Side. Alcohol
is only one of many addictions. Cigarettes, food, and activities such
as shopping, dieting, and gambling are all potentially addictive.

Compulsion. The person feels as if he or she must engage in the behavior.

Lack of Control. The person cannot stop engaging in the behavior.

Negative Consequences. The behavior is destructive to the person.

Correa explains that people suffering from addictions "continue to engage in self-destructive behavior despite the negative consequences. Their health is often affected when they drink too much or use drugs and their home life is also hurt when they injure relationships with family and friends."[1]

In this book we'll investigate addiction both in its traditional forms, such as drug and alcohol abuse, and in its broader forms, including extreme forms of behavior. What factors lead someone to become addicted? When does a healthy activity turn into a dangerous obsession? What can be done to help addicts regain control over their lives? Throughout our discussion, we'll hear about addiction from people—many of whose identities have been changed—who have experienced its consequences.

TWO
THE CAUSES AND EFFECTS OF ADDICTION

Jamie Rubin felt at home in the casinos of Atlantic City, New Jersey. For the thousands of dollars she spent playing blackjack, she enjoyed the special attention, "perks," given to "high rollers": free limousine rides, meals, and accommodations.

It seemed that Jamie led a glamorous life. A closer look revealed that things weren't so rosy. It wasn't glamour that regularly drew Jamie to the gaming tables, but a powerful addiction to gambling. To support her gambling habit, Jamie spent nearly all her money, including funds set aside for her college education. Jamie should never have been admitted to any casino: She was only seventeen years old and the legal gambling age in New Jersey was twenty-one.

When he realized what was happening, Jamie's father, an Atlantic City police detective, notified the authorities. His daughter was banned from the casinos. But it was too late. Detective Rubin said of his daughter: "She was an addicted gambler."

While casino spokespersons say that cases like Jamie's are rare, skeptics doubt this is so. Although casino security personnel in Atlantic City and elsewhere are instructed to bar minors, people who are under the legal age, it is nearly impossible to catch everyone. In the early 1990s, it was estimated that each month about 29,000 teens were turned away from the casinos in Atlantic City. Steven Perskie, chairman of New Jersey's Casino Control Commission, noted: "We can rationally assume that if we stop 29,000, then a few hundred manage to get through."[1]

Research indicates that over one million of approximately eight million compulsive gamblers in the United States are teenagers. Young people like Jamie who live near casinos can frequent them, but many others become involved in sports betting, card playing, and lotteries. "We've always seen compulsive gambling as a problem of older people," commented Jean Falzon, executive director of the National Council on Problem Gambling. "Now we are finding that adolescent compulsive gambling is far more pervasive than we had thought."[2]

It has become increasingly clear that large numbers of young people are addicted to gambling as well as to a host of other unhealthy types of behavior or substances. Why do some people become compulsive gamblers while others can limit themselves to an occasional friendly wager? What leads one person to become an addict and not another? While there are no hard and fast answers, there are some identifiable conditions of addiction.

The number of underaged gamblers is on the rise.

DISCRIMINATION

According to many individuals, social and economic inequalities have gone hand in hand with addiction. During the nineteenth century, alcoholism became a problem among Native Americans (Indians), and it continues to be today. As white Americans moved west and took control of Indian lands, the Indians were dispossessed and removed to reservations. Living conditions were poor, and education was inadequate. Despair and hopelessness, some say, drove many Indians to drink. Others charge that white Americans used alcohol as a tool to prevent Indians from resisting unfair treatment.

African Americans and Hispanics have endured discrimination, and addiction has been a problem in both communities. It's not that white Americans use fewer drugs, many say, it's that treatment programs are less widely available for people who are not white. Others add that incentives to avoid drugs—the promise of fair treatment from society and opportunities for success—are missing in black and Hispanic communities. According to Yale University historian David Musto, many people tend to think of addiction as the cause of the problems in these communities, rather than as a symptom: "That lets the rest of us off the hook, free to ignore the deeper problems of unemployment and education."[3]

Many young people rise above discrimination. Unfair treatment, however, has led some individuals to seek escape in drugs and alcohol, setting the stage for addiction.

PEER GROUP PRESSURE

While society as a whole has, according to many, contributed to addiction, smaller social groups have also played a role. Among young people, peer groups—friends, students, those of one's own age and surroundings—have a powerful influence. If a peer group values excessive behavior, drug use, or drinking, it may pressure some individuals to engage in these activities to gain acceptance. Consider the case of Jerry in Chapter One, whose dependency on alcohol began with drinking "because my friends drink at parties and it was a cool thing to do."

ADVERTISING

Advertising can also influence people to engage in activities that are potentially addictive. In 1988, for example, the R. J. Reynolds Company began to promote its Camel cigarettes using a character named Joe Camel. Some people charged that the cartoon camel was inducing younger people to smoke. Studies showed that the cigarette's popularity soared, particularly among 18- to 24-year-olds, when this advertising was introduced.[4]

HEREDITY AND FAMILY LIFE

In addition to society and peers, one's own family background can contribute to addiction. Scientists are only beginning to understand how heredity—the passing on of characteristics from parents to children—affects addiction. Mothers and fathers transmit the factors that make their offspring what they are through tiny structures in the cells called genes. Researchers have found that, in addition to features such as height and eye color, genes may determine a person's addictive tendencies. Studies show that children of alcoholic parents are four times as likely to become addicted to alcohol as other young people. The existence of a hereditary factor that contributes to

One of the many advertisements aimed at young people
features Joe Camel. A 1994 survey showed that kindergartners
found Joe Camel more recognizable than Mickey Mouse.

alcoholism was also supported by a Danish study of 5,483 adopted children. Those who had an alcoholic birth parent proved to be more prone to alcoholism when they reached adulthood. This was true even in cases where neither adoptive parent drank.[5]

While the genes a person receives from his or her biological parents play a role in addiction, the environment a person grows up in can also lead to substance abuse and uncontrolled behavior. If a parent uses alcohol or drugs or engages in some compulsive habit as a means of dealing with problems, a child may learn to imitate this behavior.

INDIVIDUAL FACTORS

All of the above factors can lead to addiction. But what of a person's own emotional makeup and choices? How can these lead a person into a destructive dependency on a drug or a habit? Let's look at some of the personality traits of those who are addicted.

Need for Perfection. Addicted individuals frequently set extremely high, often unattainable, standards for themselves. When they don't measure up to all they hoped they would be or accomplish, they become disappointed or even despairing. No one has to punish them for failing to achieve—they are extremely hard on themselves. Feeling that they are worthless, many of these individuals slide into addiction, relying on alcohol, drugs, gambling, or other destructive substances or behavior to cushion their unhappiness.

The situation is even worse when parents set nearly impossible goals for a young person and are then devastated if their child fails to fulfill their dreams. In these high-pressure environments children may be under continual stress to achieve. Searching for a release from the intense demands made on them, these young people may end up addicted. It's important to remember that not all people who have these traits or all children whose parents have very high expectations for them become addicts. A combination of factors may make one person turn to alcohol or drugs, while another person with the same traits is able to cope.

Craving Control. People who don't develop a firm inner sense of security while growing up may feel fearful and anxious. In an effort to protect themselves they may try to exert as much control as possible over various aspects of their lives. Leaving little to chance tends to make them feel safer.

Such individuals are prone to addictions. Many desperately need a release from the constant sense of threat they experience. It's not uncommon for such people to become involved in overeating, excessive shopping, gambling, or other addictions. These activities only compound their problems: An addict

Heredity can affect more than appearance. If a parent is an alcoholic, his or her children are more likely to develop an addiction to alcohol.

Teenagers who feel the need to escape from the pressures of home and school sometimes rely on alcohol to relieve stress. They risk developing a drinking problem or, worse, becoming a statistic as a drunk-driving fatality.

cannot control his or her addiction. This type of addicted person is left feeling that his or her life is even more chaotic and out of control than ever.

Overdependency. Insecurity can also lead to overdependency, another condition of addiction. It is perfectly normal for infants and children to be dependent on parents and teachers for support, care, and guidance. As children grow, they become more able to do things for themselves, and the constant assistance of others becomes less crucial. Some people, however, reach adulthood without achieving a firm sense of independence.

People who feel ill at ease without the help and assurance of others are especially vulnerable to addictive behavior. Regardless of their age, they never feel truly self-reliant. They may believe that to survive they need to cling to someone more competent and powerful than they are. To relieve the tension of feeling unable to make it on their own, such people may develop excessive habits or turn to drugs.

Denial. Overdependent people are attempting to deny their vulnerability. This denial is another practice that can lead to addiction. People who refuse to admit to powerful emotions, such as fear, anger, or rage, may find themselves becoming addicted to a substance or an activity.

Carla came from a family in which she felt that her parents always put her brother first. When there was only enough money for one of them to attend college, they sent him even though Carla was the better student. While Carla was upset, she never revealed her disappointment to her parents. Instead, she kept her resentment inside and worked evenings and weekends to earn her own money for school.

Yet Carla wasn't able to completely squelch her pain. Every time she thought about how she had been treated, the hurt and anger welled up inside her. Trying to deny that her parents cared less about her than her brother, Carla turned to alcohol. Beer and wine helped her to repress her feelings. She later claimed that drinking binges were the only times she could completely forget what growing up in her family had been like for her. Unfortunately, in the end, her alcoholism proved to be as troublesome as her painful past.

Low Self-Esteem. Many people who are addicted suffer from low self-esteem. They have a negative opinion of themselves. It may be hard to pinpoint when they started feeling this way. The feeling comes in various ways. It might be that as children they blamed themselves for their parents divorcing. Perhaps they felt worthless and unhappy after being continually criticized or ridiculed by family members or friends. In some situations, single parents may place their dating partners' needs above those of their offspring, leaving the children to deal with strong feelings of being ignored and left out of things.

Such traumatic events can convince a youth that he or she must be a bad person to have brought about such distressing circumstances. If not dealt with early on, these feelings can persist and grow through the years. Although as teenagers or adults the individuals may understand that they weren't responsible for what happened during childhood, guilt and a wish for self-punishment may persist. Individuals with little regard for

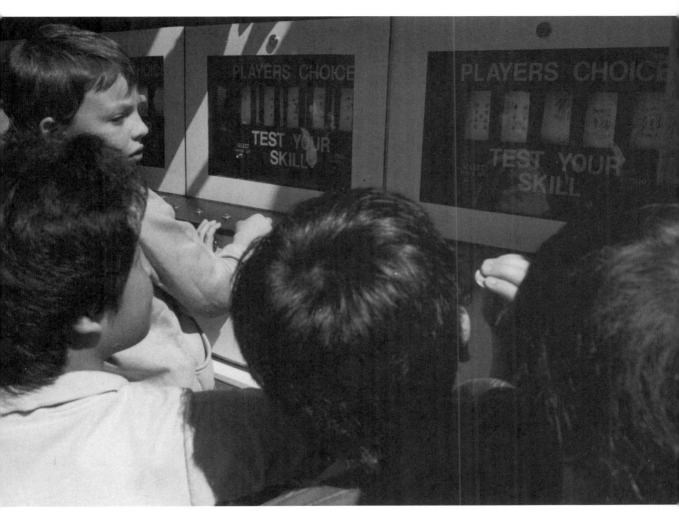

Although these boys are only placing small bets at a fair, the potential outcome is a gambling habit that could last a lifetime and cost thousands of dollars.

themselves sometimes become involved in self-destructive behaviors such as addictions.

THE EFFECTS OF ADDICTION

Regardless of what may cause someone to become addicted, both the person and society suffer. Michael, a Boston teenager addicted to gambling, began playing cards with his friends for money. Before long, he stole cash from his mother's wallet to help support his gambling habit. As he grew older, he bet on sports events and eventually began playing in Atlantic City casinos. By the time he was in his early twenties, he had been arrested for embezzlement and for stealing a woman's purse.

Similar stories of the destructive effects of addiction are common. In the late 1980s several members of a Dallas, Texas, state champion high school football team and their friends received stiff prison sentences for a series of armed robberies staged to pay their gambling debts. The boys had become involved in high-stakes dice games at their school. Other teens have been arrested and convicted for robberies carried out to support their alcohol and drug habits. Alcohol abuse also accounts for 42 percent of all fatal alcohol-related automobile crashes in which the driver was under eighteen.[6]

Addictions tend to be costly in more personal ways as well. The more severe the addiction, the more isolated the person usually becomes from family and friends. At times, he or she may grow distant and secretive in an effort to hide the problem. Those closest to the person may find that they now come second after the substance or compulsion that dominates the addict's life. The person who is addicted may even take up with a new group of friends involved in the same addictive behavior.

Before long, school, sports, or other activities that were important to the person before his or her addiction fade into the background. In such situations, it's not uncommon for formerly good students to receive failing grades.

Addiction is quite clearly a tragic and destructive form of behavior. Nevertheless, there are some addictions that are reinforced by society, friends, and family.

Studying is an excellent habit, but when done to
excess, it, too, can turn into an addiction.

THREE

HOW CAN SOMETHING THAT'S GOOD BE BAD?

CATLIN / AGE 15

"I go to a very competitive school, the kind of place where the 'dumb' kids get B's. At assemblies our dean tells us we're special; we're tomorrow's leaders. We're expected to strive for excellence in everything we do. My parents say that they expect me to succeed too. I grew up that way—all the kids in my family did. My brother and sister really took their lectures seriously. My brother got straight A's in school. My sister's a brain too.

"I am the youngest. I had to follow those two all through school, so I was used to teachers asking if I was as smart as my brother and sister. The truth is I'm not; school was always much harder for me.

"For a long time, my main goal was not to disappoint my parents. I saw how proud they were of my brother and sister. I didn't want to be the kid they were ashamed of, the one they wished they'd never had.

"So I studied. I think I studied more than any kid I knew. I gave up going out with my friends after school and on weekends to spend more time at the library. I even stopped seeing a boy I liked because he was distracting me. We tried having study dates but we never got much studying done. He didn't understand why I was so worried about school—he always wanted to be out with our friends. I felt that I couldn't have a boyfriend or girlfriends until I was getting straight A's, and I was a long way from that. It's hard to have a good time when your mind's on a test you've taken or a paper that's due.

"My parents tried to help. My Mom gave up outings with her friends so she could drive me back and forth from the library. She went out of her way to get materials for my science projects too. I did my part by trying harder in school.

"The results were worth the work. My grades went up in everything but math, and my teachers were impressed. I became determined never to be outside the 'smart circle' again.

"I started studying like a crazy person. Instead of going to the beach that summer I stayed in my room and read the books on our fall reading list. I did well that semester, but I still worried about my grades going down. It got so bad that I'd get this terrible burning pain in my stomach. My mother took me to a doctor who told me to take it easy. He said that otherwise I could get an ulcer. But I wasn't going to study less. I had come too far. Letting up even just a little could cost me a lot—too much as far as I was concerned."

DRIVEN TO DESTRUCTION

Catlin studied compulsively. She believed that unless she was a straight-A student, she could not feel good about herself. Even though Catlin's behavior deprived her of many of the pleasures and relationships of a well-rounded person, she was nevertheless rewarded for her effort and achievement. Some therapists would call Catlin's persistence and drive a positive or "applauded" addiction.[1] Applauded addictions are types of behavior that are often admired by others. When these ways of behaving are compulsively carried to an extreme, however, they can be just as destructive as a drug or alcohol addiction.

One of the obstacles in overcoming applauded addictions, as well as other addictions, is recognizing the problem. Individuals who study too many hours or train too hard for a particular sport are frequently seen as dedicated and committed to a goal. The support and admiration they receive from others only make it more difficult for such people to give up what is actually a draining addiction.

Without some type of intervention, such individuals may soon reach their breaking point. As mental-health experts point out in the book *We Are Driven: The Compulsive Behaviors America Applauds,* "the old complaint 'This job is going to be the death of me' contains a lot of truth. Not only is physical ailment a constant threat to the hard-charging perfectionist, but he or she also runs the risk of serious mental fatigue. . . . Many patients . . . describe symptoms of anxiety or depression that sap their energy and effectiveness. In our counseling sessions, as we unravel what is going on behind the symptoms, we discover people who simply have pushed themselves to a snapping point."[2]

People with applauded addictions fit many of the categories leading to addiction described in Chapter Two. But unlike people addicted to alcohol or cocaine, individuals with applauded addictions feel that they must prove their worth every day. To meet an important deadline or achieve a specific goal, anyone might overextend herself or himself at any time. Driven people, though, don't shut down once the crisis is over. Even when these individuals do well, they frequently feel they should have accomplished more and criticize themselves for not doing better. The unstated motto of such perfectionists is usually, "Do more and be more. More is always better."[3] People with applauded addictions feel they must be perfect.

That was the case with Bryana, the youngest of four children and the only girl in her family. Bryana learned to skate shortly after she began walking. The cold winters of her small New England town provided an ideal climate for the sport, and Bryana had a flair for it. Before long, people said she displayed unusual style and grace on the ice for a child her age. Bryana began taking private figure-skating lessons, and by the time she was seven her coach predicted that one day she'd skate in the Olympics.

Bryana's mother, a seamstress who made costumes for local skating productions, had once hoped to become an outstanding figure skater. She never achieved that goal but was thrilled at the thought that her daughter might. Bryana's father was pleased as well and even took a second job to help cover his daughter's skating expenses.

The financial and emotional support provided by Bryana's family placed a heavy burden on the young girl. She felt she owed it to her parents to do well. Yet pleasing her family was only part of why Bryana strove to be the best. She savored the satisfaction of mastering difficult skating routines and enjoyed winning as the crowd cheered her on. At just ten years of age, Bryana felt nothing in her future was as important as skating.

Compulsive behavior may begin on the athletic field or
in the classroom, but it often leads to more destructive
addictions, such as to alcohol or drugs.

On most days she spent more than eight hours practicing. Bryana didn't have time for clubs or any sort of after-school activities. Her only friends were the people she met skating, and they were more like acquaintances than real companions. She never went to movies, parties, or malls with people her age. But Bryana felt skating was worth the sacrifice.

Her intense dedication to the sport was obvious in other ways as well. Prior to a competition she always put in more practice time than her coach thought necessary, even leaving school early to work in extra sessions. Once she even lied to her coach and parents about a painful leg injury so she'd be allowed to skate. Bryana also continually dieted to look good in her skating costumes. She'd force herself to skip snacks regardless of how hungry she was or how thin she'd become.

At first Bryana's hard work seemed to pay off. She starred in the town's skating shows and frequently took first or second place in local competitions. The town newspaper wrote favorably about her, while the younger skaters idolized her. But as Bryana started participating in state and regional competitions, things began to change. Her coach wasn't sure whether Bryana's skills were inferior to those of other top skaters or if she just had competition jitters. But either way, she usually did poorly in these trials.

Claiming that she'd worked too hard to just give up, the determined skater swore she'd turn things around. Bryana began practicing longer hours than ever. She even saw a therapist to learn relaxation techniques for major competitions. But despite her best efforts, Bryana showed little improvement over the months.

Her parents and coach finally realized that their Olympic hopeful would probably never be more than the hometown skating queen. Now they encouraged Bryana to view skating as a hobby and develop other interests. She tried but found this nearly impossible to do. She made some friends at school, yet when she was with them she wished she were skating.

Bryana continued to spend at least four hours a day on the ice. She knew she'd never skate professionally but liked the way gliding across a lake or skating rink made her feel. She also admitted that she still enjoyed the admiring glances of on-lookers. Bryana later told a counselor that she sometimes wondered if she'd ever be like other people. She simply felt that skating was in her blood.

PAID TO PERFORM

Although young people are driven by applauded addictions, the problem is also common among adults. It can be even more difficult to solve in these cases since people with applauded addictions often find jobs that pay them for their dependency.

While people with applauded addictions can be found in any profession, research has revealed that, as adults, such individuals tend to enter three types of professions. Some become entrepreneurs, or independent business owners. Often such individuals start a business from scratch and work day and night to make it grow. If they succeed, they are frequently looked upon as self-made men or women—but they never let up on themselves.

Others with applauded addictions work in corporations as high-level executives. They may hold key positions in marketing, administration, or sales. Generally, these employees are known for their drive, and they are regarded as company "movers and shakers."

The third career category to which people with applauded addictions are drawn is the "helping or rescuing" professions. These include the ministry, teaching, social work, counseling, and medicine. Compulsively driven individuals in these fields tend to work selflessly and seemingly endlessly for others. Usually, they work considerably harder than their colleagues, extending themselves to go "that extra mile."

No matter what profession they choose, such ultimate achievers frequently arrive early at work, leave late, and take their responsibilities seriously. To some people they appear to be models of perfection. Yet beneath the surface, they are consumed with proving to themselves and to the rest of the world that they are productive and worthwhile human beings. However, it's important to remember that not everyone who works hard to start a business or advance in a company or helping profession is engaging in addictive behavior. A person crosses the line when work becomes all-consuming and destructive, and the person feels that he or she still can't let up.

FOUR
RECOVERY

The first step in trying to recover from any addiction is for people to recognize that they have a problem. Recovery from an addiction, whether it is an applauded addiction or one that is shunned by society, is never easy. Many methods have been used to end dependency. Some have been used often and have proven successful. Others are controversial. The path out of dependency can be filled with pitfalls.

COLD TURKEY

Some people who are addicted simply force themselves to stop taking the drug or engaging in the destructive behavior. This is called going "cold turkey." Smokers have kicked their dependency on nicotine—the addictive ingredient in tobacco—simply by tossing their cigarettes in the trash and gritting their teeth until their physical and psychological needs for the drug are broken. Others have tried this method and failed.

There are people who say that the "cold turkey" way of dealing with addiction ignores its underlying causes. They say it can lead addicts out of one addiction and right into another. In fact, research has shown that between 40 and 75 percent of people who enter treatment programs have been involved in multiple addictions.

One incident of cross-addiction that received widespread media attention involved Kitty Dukakis, the wife of Michael Dukakis, the former governor of Massachusetts and the Democratic party's presidential nominee in 1988. During her husband's campaign, Kitty Dukakis publicly acknowledged that she had been addicted to diet pills [amphetamines] for a number of years. The would-be First Lady assured the public that she had conquered the addiction and made a full recovery. Yet just two years later, she announced that she was battling a second addiction—alcoholism. She entered a treatment center, and, several weeks later, again claimed that she had recovered.

Afterward, Kitty Dukakis embarked on a national crusade against substance abuse. She traveled extensively throughout the nation to spread the word. Yet the flurry of activity appeared to leave little time for her to work through what had initially led her into two addictions. Unfortunately, before long things took a turn for the worse. Just a few months after leaving the alcohol treatment center, she was rushed to a Boston hospital for emergency care. In a desperate moment she had drunk

Kitty Dukakis, who received treatment for alcoholism, travels throughout the world speaking about the dangers of addiction and encouraging others to reach out for help.

SPORTS AND ALCOHOL DON'T MIX

FOUNDATION•Poster designed by Linda Cheung, Age 18, Toronto

SED

Alcohol.
You have a choice.

Ministry of Health

Alcohol and Drug
Programs

**No alcohol
for our baby.**

Alcohol.
You have a choice

rubbing alcohol in combination with an antidepressant medication she was taking. Kitty Dukakis survived, but it was clear that she had to resolve the causes of her addiction.[1]

INTERVENTION

In treating addictions, quick fixes rarely bring long-term cures. Before any meaningful change can occur, many experts say the person must break through the wall of denial that frequently surrounds those who have an addiction and admit there's a problem. This may be difficult because addictions themselves often serve as protective shields against pain and turmoil.

To convince addicts that something is terribly wrong and that they need help, a process known as intervention may be used. During an intervention family members and close friends of such persons confront them with the truth about their behavior. They fend off denials and excuses by citing precise incidents when the addiction caused problems and misery for both the addicts and their loved ones.

Bombarded by the evidence presented, addicts eventually admit that all the important people in their lives can't be wrong. At that point those who are present assure such individuals that they will support them and assist in getting help. Then they discuss the various treatment options. To be a positive experience, an intervention must be carefully planned and carried out under the supervision of a trained therapist in the field.

At first glance, intervention may seem unfair to the ones who are addicted. Such individuals are outnumbered and made to face humiliating truths. Intervention's purpose is not to shame them but to break through their defenses so that they will get the needed help.

There are those who have been critical of intervention and consider it a cruel process. Courtney Love, wife of Kurt Cobain, leader of the rock group Nirvana, arranged an intervention to confront her husband with his heroin addiction. Following the intervention, Cobain checked into a treatment center, only to check out a few days later. He eventually committed suicide. Love said later that she regretted putting her husband through the ordeal of intervention.

Once people admit to an addiction, there are various forms of medical and professional assistance available.

MEDICAL AND PROFESSIONAL HELP

Some who are addicted work with doctors, social workers, or mental health counselors in an office setting, a hospital, or a mental health or addiction treatment center. Depending on the person's needs and the nature of the addiction, the individual may either begin an inpatient or outpatient treatment program. With inpatient treatment, the individual enters a facility and lives in a drug-free environment with the support of a professional medical staff and other recovering patients. Depending on the treatment plan and the underlying cause of the addiction, the person may be given medication. Usually the person attends both individual and group counseling sessions and eventually leaves the center with a plan to continue working on recovery. After going home, the person usually returns for weekly counseling sessions for a period of time.

In outpatient treatment, the individual continues to live at home, but visits a doctor's office, hospital, or clinic for individual and group therapy sessions. Depending upon the particular case, family therapy involving the person's immediate and extended family may be necessary as well.

TWELVE-STEP PROGRAMS

In overcoming addictions, some people prefer self-help programs. Among the oldest and best known of such routes to recovery are twelve-step programs. Alcoholics Anonymous (AA), Overeaters Anonymous (OA), and Gamblers Anonymous (GA), among others, are all twelve-step programs.

These programs generally assume that people are primarily responsible for their own addictions. They acknowledge that outside influences may have played an important role in encouraging addiction, but those who support this process insist that ultimately the addicted person made a choice to respond to these influences by turning to drugs or some other destructive activity. Only by facing the addiction can the person be helped.

Participants face their addictions by taking twelve specific steps; hence the program's name. William Wilson, a stockbroker, and Robert Smith, a doctor, developed the twelve steps in 1935. Both men were alcoholics seeking a way out of their ad-

Kurt Cobain, lead singer of the rock group Nirvana, committed suicide in 1994 after years of addiction to alcohol and drugs.

Counseling sessions can be very helpful
to teens in overcoming their addictions.

diction. Their method was successful for them and was soon used by others. Their original twelve steps are:

We—

1. Admitted we were powerless over alcohol—that our lives had become unmanageable
2. Came to believe that a Power greater than ourselves could restore us to sanity
3. Made a decision to turn our will and our lives over to the care of God as we understood Him
4. Made a searching and fearless moral inventory of ourselves
5. Admitted to God, to ourselves, and to another human being the exact nature of our wrongs
6. Were entirely ready to have God remove all these defects of character
7. Humbly asked Him to remove our shortcomings
8. Made a list of the persons we harmed, and became willing to make amends to them all
9. Made direct amends to such people wherever possible, except when to do so would injure them or others
10. Continued to take personal inventory and when we were wrong promptly admitted it
11. Sought through prayer and meditation to improve our conscious contact with God as we understood Him, praying only for knowledge of His will for us and the power to carry that out
12. Having had a spiritual awakening as the result of these steps, we tried to carry this message to alcoholics, and to practice these principles in all our affairs

These steps have since been adapted for a variety of programs. No matter what their slant, however, all twelve-step programs require people to stop taking the drug or engaging in the activity to which they are addicted. In addition, participants attend regular meetings in which they share their experiences with others. Many people swear by the twelve-step method and, indeed, it has been shown to help millions. Others say that one of its basic assumptions—once an addict, always an addict—ignores people's ability to change.

A DIFFICULT JOURNEY

No matter what type of treatment is chosen, recovering from an addiction can be a long and difficult journey. The recovery route rarely follows a straight path. Encouraging moments and disappointing setbacks occur along the way. While the help and support of family members are often essential, at times these individuals may feel emotionally drained themselves. Fortunately, many self-help groups offer related support groups for the addicted person's family. Families receiving professional help may also seek counseling to assist them in dealing with problems that arise.

Recovering from an addiction is easier when everyone involved is honest, open, and willing to face possibly stressful incidents and relationships. Although some people may be ashamed to admit they have an addiction, needing help should not be embarrassing. It takes strength and courage to tackle a difficult problem, and those who do so deserve respect and support.

One young woman addicted to overeating described her feelings this way:

"It took me a long time to admit that I was out of control when it came to food. I'd tell myself that I could stop overeating if I just tried hard enough. But it never really worked. I'd want to die after binging, so I'd starve myself for the next few days. But I overate more than I starved, so I always looked heavy. That's when I'd tell people that I had a glandular problem or that I was taking medication that made me gain weight.

"A therapist once told me that addictions are medical problems that require treatment. But it's hard to say you have that kind of problem. If you broke your arm, you wouldn't think twice about having the bones set and wearing a cast. You wouldn't feel ashamed or try to hide it. An addiction really isn't much different. Isn't the mind as much a part of the body as an arm or leg?

"I'm getting the help I need now. It's hard, but I know I'm worth the work ahead. I always thought of food as my retreat, but I was also punishing myself with it. I still have a long way to go, but I'm glad I took this step."

NOTES

CHAPTER ONE   1. "Addictive Disorders Reap Millions," *USA Today* (January 1992), p.5.

CHAPTER TWO   1. Ricardo Chavira, "The Rise of Teenage Gambling," *Time* (February 25, 1991), p.78.
2. Ibid.
3. David Musto, *Time* (December 3, 1990), p.47.
4. Patricia M. Tice, "The Drug Culture," in *Altered States* (Rochester, NY: The Strong Museum, 1992), p.121.
5. Paula Dranov, "The Harrowing Mystery of Addiction," *Cosmopolitan* (July 1988), p.150.
6. David Elkind, "Drug Abuse and Teenagers," *Parents* (February 1987), p.164.

CHAPTER THREE   1. Dr. Robert Hemfelt, Dr. Frank Minirth, and Dr. Paul Meier, *We Are Driven: The Compulsive Behaviors America Applauds* (Nashville, TN: Thomas Nelson Publishers, 1991), p.8.
2. Ibid, p.10.
3. Ibid, p.21.

CHAPTER FOUR   1. Anastasia Toufexis, "The Struggle Of Kitty Dukakis," *Time* (February 20, 1989), p.79.

FURTHER INFORMATION

Al-Anon Family Group Headquarters
P.O. Box 862, Midtown Station
New York, NY 10018

Alcohol and Drug Problems
Association of North America
444 N. Capitol Street NW, Suite 706
Washington, DC 20001

Alcoholics Anonymous World Service
475 Riverside Drive
New York, NY 10163

American Council For Drug Education
204 Monroe Street, Suite 110
Rockville, MD 20850

American Council On Alcoholism
White Marsh Business Center
5024 Campbell Boulevard, Suite H
Baltimore, MD 21236

Cocaine Anonymous World Service
3740 Overland Avenue, Suite G
Los Angeles, CA 90034

Co-Dependents Anonymous
P.O. Box 33577
Phoenix, AZ 85067-3577

Debtors Anonymous
P.O. Box 20322
New York, NY 10025-9992

Gamblers Anonymous (GA)
P.O. Box 17173
Los Angeles, CA 90017

Narcotics Anonymous
P.O. Box 9999
Van Nuys, CA 91409

Narcotics Education, Inc.
55 W. Oakridge Drive
Hagerstown, MD 21740

National Association
For Children Of Alcoholics
(NACOA)
11426 Rockville Pike, Suite 100
Rockville, MD 20852

National Council on
Alcoholism and Drug Dependence
12 W. 21st Street
New York, NY 10010

National Self-Help Clearinghouse
25 W. 43d Street, Room 620
New York, NY 10036

Overachievers Anonymous
1766 Union Street, Suite C
San Francisco, CA 94123

Overeaters Anonymous
4025 Spencer Street, Suite 203
Torrance, CA 90503

Stop Teen-Age Addiction to Tobacco
121 Lyman Street, Suite 210
Springfield, MA 01103

FURTHER READING

Berger, Gilda. *Joey's Story: Straight Talk About Drugs.* Brookfield, CT: The Millbrook Press, 1991.

Berger, Gilda. *Patty's Story: Straight Talk About Drugs.* Brookfield, CT: The Millbrook Press, 1991.

Bode, Janet. *Beating the Odds: Stories of Unexpected Achievers.* New York: Franklin Watts, 1991.

Cheney, Glenn Alan. *Drugs, Teens, and Recovery: Real Life Stories of Trying to Stay Clean.* Hillside, NJ: Enslow Publishers, 1993.

Clayton, Lawrence. *Coping with a Drug Abusing Parent.* New York: Rosen, 1991.

DeStefano, Susan. *Drugs and the Family.* New York: Twenty-first Century Books, 1991.

Harris, Jonathan. *Drugged America.* New York: Four Winds, 1991.

Haubrich-Casperson, Jane, and Doug Van Nispen. *Coping with Teenage Gambling.* New York: Rosen, 1993.

Hurwitz, Ann Ricki and Sue H. *Hallucinogens.* New York: Rosen, 1992.

Hyde, Margaret O. *Know About Drugs.* New York: Walker, 1990.

Johnson, Joan J. *America's War on Drugs.* New York: Franklin Watts, 1990.

Landau, Elaine. *Weight: A Teenage Concern.* New York: Lodestar, 1991.

Moe, Barbara. *Coping with Eating Disorders.* New York: Rosen, 1991.

Schulman, Jeffrey. *Drugs and Crime.* New York: Twenty-first Century Books, 1991.

Septian, Al. *Everything You Need to Know About Codependency.* New York: Rosen, 1993.

Silverstein, Alvin, Virginia, and Robert. *The Addictions Handbook.* Hillside, NJ: Enslow Publishers, 1991.

Silverstein, Herma. *Alcoholism.* New York: Franklin Watts, 1990.

Sonder, Ben. *Eating Disorders: When Food Turns Against You.* New York: Franklin Watts, 1993.

INDEX

Page numbers in *italics* refer to illustrations.

DATE DUE			